© Published by Peter Haddock Ltd., Bridlington,
England. Printed in China.

SANTA'S SUPER SLEIGH

Written & Illustrated by John Patience

Santa had settled down by the fireside after a hard day's toy-making.

"Reindeer are old-fashioned," he said. "They are a thing of the past. It's time I went in for something more technological."

"What on earth are you talking about?" said Mrs Claus.

"I'm replacing Rudolf and the others with a Super Sleigh," said Santa. "It's advertised in this Autosleigh magazine. I've sent away for it."

"This looks like trouble to me," thought Mrs Claus.

The Super Sleigh came in kit form. Santa and his elves had some difficulty understanding the instructions but, eventually, they managed to put it together.

"You seem to have one or two pieces left over," said Mrs Claus.

"Yes, that's true," admitted Santa, "but I don't suppose they are important. It looks wonderful, don't you think?"

"Mmmm," said Mrs Claus. "You wouldn't get me up in a thing like that!"

It was Christmas Eve and Santa and his elves were loading the Super Sleigh. Rudolf and the other reindeer looked on, feeling sad and unwanted.

"I'm sorry," said Santa. "I know you love to pull the sleigh, but I can't deliver computer games and the like on a sleigh pulled by reindeer, now can I?"

Santa climbed into the Super Sleigh and pressed the starting button. The engine roared into and away he flew.

"Never mind, Rudolf," said M Claus. "I still love you."

The Super Sleigh was fantastic!
Santa zoomed around the world
getting through his deliveries in
record time. America, Russia,
Paris, Egypt and Italy all went by
in a flash.

Santa was flying over Britain when
suddenly the engine gave an
enormous BANG and the sleigh
began to loop the loop.

"Help!" cried Santa. "I'm out of
control!"

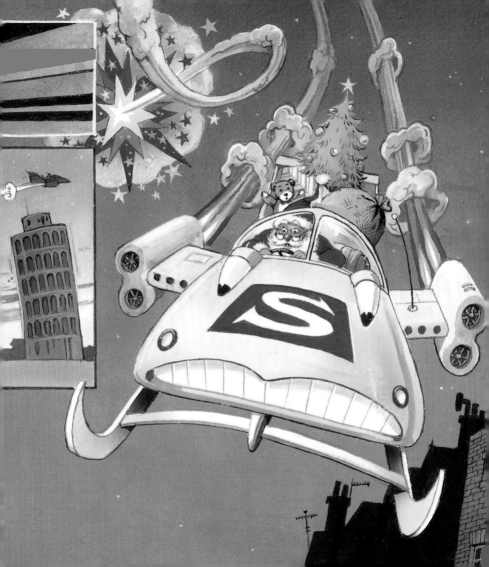

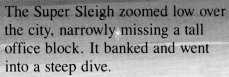

The Super Sleigh zoomed low over
the city, narrowly missing a tall
office block. It banked and went
into a steep dive.
 "Oh, help!" cried Santa,
covering his eyes. "I can't look!"
Could this be the end for Santa?
The Super Sleigh ploughed into
something soft and cold – a great,
big snowman – and Santa was
thrown high into the air!

Dazed but unhurt, Santa stood up and brushed the snow off his red suit. He was in the middle of a public park and unfortunately the gates were locked. There was nothing for it but to climb over. Well, Santa was old and fat and not used to climbing and he got stuck. It was an hour before a policeman came along and found him there, and it took some explaining!

"I'll let you go with a caution this time," said the policeman, "but drive your sleigh more carefully next time."

Santa said he certainly would and went off to telephone Mrs Claus at the North Pole. Mrs Claus was in the barn feeding the reindeer. They all had a good laugh at Santa's story.

"Don't worry," she giggled. "We'll rescue you."

Mrs Claus soon had the reindeer hitched up to the old sleigh. She flew out to help poor, old Santa and that was how the rest of the Christmas presents were delivered; the good, old-fashioned way.

"There'll be no more Super Sleighs for me!" laughed Santa as they flew home. "How about robot reindeer? Only kidding, Rudolf! Ho, ho, ho!"